Feb 2017

COCO
BUTTERNUT

COCO BUTTERNUT

A HAP AND LEONARD ADVENTURE

JOE R. LANSDALE

SUBTERRANEAN PRESS 2017

First Edition

ISBN
978-1-59606-803-2

Subterranean Press
PO Box 190106
Burton, MI 48519

subterraneanpress.com

for Bill Crider

*"Heaven goes by favor. If it went by merit,
you would stay out and your dog would go in."*
Mark Twain

"ALL I WANT you to do is make the exchange. Give them the bag, and they'll give you Coco Butternut."

We were all in the office of Brett Sawyer's Investigations, me and Leonard and Brett, my daughter Chance, and this little, chubby guy, Jimmy Farmer who wore a very bad toupée. He wanted us to make an exchange for him. Give some blackmailer a bag full of money in exchange for a dog called Coco Butternut that had belonged to Farmer's mother, as did the pet cemetery, a mortuary, and a cemetery for humans called Oak Rest.

Our German shepherd, Buffy, was also present, lying on the couch, about as interested as a dog can be in conversations that don't involve the words "treat" or "outside."

What was odd about all this was Coco Butternut was as dead as a stone and mummified.

"Let me see here," Leonard said. "You got a pickled dog stolen from you, and you want us to give some money to a guy that dug him up—"

"Her," Jimmy said. He had a condescending way of talking and a face that somehow made you want to punch it. He had all the personality of the Ebola virus. I hadn't liked him on sight, and I wasn't sure why.

"Okay," Leonard said. "Her. You want us to give a bag of money to a dead dog–napper and he gives us the mutt, and that's it?"

"That's all," Farmer said. "Only one of you can do it. He said to send one person to make the exchange. He said I could do it, but I'm not comfortable with that, and I told him so."

"You two talked person to person?" Brett said.

"No, we... Does this girl work here?"

"That's my daughter, Chance," I said. He had been eyeing her since he first came in, as if she might have designs on his wallet.

"She can be discreet?" he said.

"She certainly can," Chance said. Chance had her thick black hair tied back in a ponytail, and she was dressed the same as Brett, tee-shirt and blue-jeans and tennis shoes. She looked like a fifties teeny bopper. Even in her twenties she could have easily passed for eighteen or nineteen. She was so sweet she broke my heart.

Farmer paused a moment, taking time to consider how discreet Chance could be, I suppose.

"Okay," he said. "This thief, we didn't talk face to face. First he sent me a note that said he had the dog.

I went to the pet cemetery to look. There was a hole where she was buried, an empty grave. No question the body was gone.

"There was a sealed plastic bag in the empty grave. Inside of it was a burner phone. There was a note with a number on it. I called the number. That's how we spoke, and that's when he told me what he wanted. I threw the phone away like he asked."

"You know the man's voice?" Leonard asked.

"No. It may even have not been a man."

"You keep saying he," I said.

"Look, it was one of those synthesizer things. You can't tell who you're talking to. Sounds more male than female on those things. I couldn't tell the sex or age really. Voice said they had my mother's dog, and he wanted money."

"They?" Brett asked.

"What the voice said."

"Why was the dog pickled?" Leonard said.

"Embalmed and wrapped like a mummy," Farmer said. "Not pickled."

"Same thing," Leonard said. "Except for the duct tape."

"No tape. Cloth. Mother had it done five years ago. She died shortly thereafter. The wrapping is stuck to the dog with some kind of adhesive. They embalmed her, and then wrapped her. It's not duct tape."

"Can I ask why?" I said.

"We own a pet mortuary and cemetery. Most dogs are cremated, but we offer a variety of services. Embalming and mummification for example. Coco Butternut was a show dog. A dachshund. She had won a number of dog show awards. Nothing big, but Mother adored her. She had all her dogs embalmed. Coco Butternut was the first one to be wrapped, mummified."

"I know we can become very attached to our pets," Brett said. "But it isn't your dog, and well, it's dead. You sure you want to pay for a mummified dog corpse?"

"I never really cared for the dog," Farmer said. "It bit me a few times. Nasty animal. But Mother was sentimental about it, and I'm sentimental about her. The dog meant a lot to her."

I didn't actually find Farmer all that sentimental, but you never really know someone at first blush, and truth is, you may not ever know someone even when you think you do.

"When you say a lot," Leonard said, "the next question is how much is this sentiment going to cost you?"

"I'd rather not say. Just deliver the bag and bring home the dog."

"I got one more question," Leonard said. "Who names a dog Coco Butternut?"

"Mother," Farmer said.

"Not to step on your mother's grave, but why the hell would she name a dog that," Leonard said. "She just go by Coco, or Butter, or Nut?"

"Dog had a chocolate body, but butternut colored paws. That's how the name came about."

"Could have just called her Spot, or Socks or some such," Leonard said. "Hell, Trixie. I had a dog named Trixie. That's a good name."

FARMER WAS PAYING us good money to deliver the bag, and the good money was considerably more than what we normally made for a few hours' work. He really wanted that dog back.

Plan was I would make the drop and exchange, and Leonard would find a place to hide in case things went south. We weren't hired to take the body snatcher down, and in fact, Farmer insisted we didn't. Said things could go wrong if we tried to do that. Thing was make the exchange and keep it smooth and simple.

Leonard went over to Farmer's house, picked up the money and was bringing it to us. I was looking out the office window as he drove up. It was a nice spring day and bright and the young woman downstairs that owned the bicycle shop was wearing shorts and her legs were long and brown and Brett wasn't looking at me right then and Chance was sorting out the lunch she had picked up from a Japanese restaurant. Buffy was watching me, but she didn't care what I was doing.

I kept a steady vigil as the fine looking shop owner leaned over a bike she was repairing. Those shorts certainly could ride high.

It wasn't that I wasn't fine with my woman. I'm a one-woman man. But I still like to look. I think it's good for my heart or something, maybe even the liver.

Leonard parked and came across the lot, nodding at the blonde as he did. He looked up and saw me at the window and smiled. He came up the stairs and inside and placed the satchel on the desk. It had a clasp lock on it with a ring and through the ring was a tiny padlock.

Leonard said, "Brett, I think Hap was looking at that blonde's butt out there."

"Daddy," Chance said.

"I was merely looking out the window," I said.

"I've noticed you do that a lot when she's out there," Brett said. "Don't con me, Hap Collins."

"Okay, the con is over," I said. "So I can look at will?"

"I didn't say that," Brett said. "I prefer you think you're being sneaky. It shows you have some pride."

"That's one way of looking at it," Leonard said. "Now, you all thinking what I'm thinking?"

"How much money is in that bag," I said.

"That's right," Leonard said.

"We don't need to know," Brett said. "And besides, it's locked."

"Hap's going into this with a bag of money, someone bringing a dead dog to him. I think it might be wise to see how much is in the bag. I don't like that Farmer guy, anyway."

Brett came over and looked down at the satchel. "Like I said. We don't need to know. But, my lock-pick kit is in the drawer."

Chance opened the drawer and removed the kit, handed it to Brett. She took out her tools and worked on the lock for a moment or two. It clicked open.

"He gave me a key to give to the kidnapper," Leonard said. "But I just wanted to see you work that lock."

Brett grinned at Leonard. "You rascal."

"And then some," Leonard said.

Brett opened the satchel. There were a lot of bills in it, stacks bound by paper binders. She took it out and thumbed through it.

"Jesus," she said. "There's something like a hundred thousand dollars here."

"For a dead dog?" Leonard said.

"This guy must be rich," Chance said.

"He is. Should have seen his house. You could park my apartment, your house, and this building in it. Well, there might not be room for the couch."

"Ha," I said.

"Yeah," Leonard said, "that putting dead bodies in the ground pays mighty good."

Brett said, "Now we know," closed the satchel and put the lock back on it.

WE DECIDED FIRST to have a recon mission before we made the actual drop. The team, as I like to think of us, drove out to the drop spot. That means me and Leonard, Brett and Chance. Chance decided she wanted to get in on things, and we decided to let her, as long as it wasn't dangerous. It was pretty much a family business, so why not.

Drop was to take place at a graveyard, which when you think about it is kind of ironic. Dog was dug up from a graveyard, and was to be returned in one.

This one was an old graveyard for black citizens. It was called the Colored Graveyard by some, and there was a historical marker that called it a Negro Graveyard. It stopped being used mid-twentieth century, and though it was kept up, it was a piss-poor job. Someone hacked the weeds around the graves now and then with what appeared to be a stick. The drop was to happen at a grave for K. Hollis Colby. It was one of the few tombstones that was still intact. It was the only large tombstone and it was one of the few where you could see the name clearly on it. The dates of birth and death were not so clear. Looking at it I thought no matter who you are or where you are or when you're from, time passes away, and so do you and the memory of you. Maybe someone keeps it alive for a few generations, but most of us aren't remembered after the last shovelful of dirt is thrown in the hole.

"So this kidnapper's supposed to bring Coco Butterbutt here," Leonard said.

"Butternut," I said.

"I know. I just don't like that guy, and by proxy I think his dog is an asshole. Who names a fucking dog Coco Butternut?"

"His mother," I said.

"The dog's mother?"

"Now you're being a jerk. Farmer's mother."

"What kind of mother does that? Gives a dog a name like that."

Chance was coming across the graveyard to meet us. She had a device in her hand.

When she came up, she said, "Kind of sad here, isn't it?"

"Oh, I don't know," Leonard said. "They're dead. I'm kind of over it."

"Leonard," Chance said, "you are a turd."

"Just a little bit," he said, and tipped his fedora back. He had taken to wearing it all the time. It wasn't a hat that irritated me, like some he wore. That goddamn deerstalker I took care of, and I don't think he even missed it, which means he merely had it to mess with me. He walked around in that thing, strutting like a peacock, drawing attention to himself because he knew that drew attention to me, and he knew it embarrassed me to be seen with him in that damn thing. The fedora. That was cool.

"Brett said you have to find some place to put this it can't be seen. It picks up voices good. You plant it, and we'll be back across the way, and we can hear everything."

"Where you'll be," Leonard said, "something goes down, by the time you or Brett get here with a big ole pistol or a long stick, Hap'll be dead and bleeding on ole Colby here."

"Don't be so morbid," Chance said. "He'll be all right. He's got you closer by."

"Girl, you are what we call a goddamn optimist," Leonard said. "You ain't been around your dad enough to know trouble follows his ass around."

"Maybe it's you trouble follows," Chance said. "You two are always together."

"Might be something to that," Leonard said.

There was a thin pine sapling that had grown up in the graveyard, and it wasn't far from the grave where we were supposed to make the exchange.

"Put it there," I said.

Chance went over to the sapling and Leonard walked over to help her. I stood where I was thinking something about this whole thing smelled like the ass end of a dead elephant. Outside of what we were being asked to do, something else wasn't right.

"We got it," Chance said.

"I think I actually got it," Leonard said.

"I held it while you fastened it down," she said.

"Yeah, but I turned it on," Leonard said.

"Children," I said. "Back to the car."

∽∘∾

DRIVING US BACK to the office, Brett said, "We'll get there before dark so Leonard can hide in the woods. He's got a mike, and I got one. We can both hear what's going down and Leonard will be close if something turns sideways."

"I can hear it too," Chance said.

"Of course you can," Leonard said.

"Uncle Leonard," Chance said. "I am going to hit you in the eye."

Leonard laughed. "You are my kind of kid."

"I'm not a kid."

"Of course you aren't," Leonard said. "You are in your twenties, and therefore you are grown and know all there is to know."

Chance was in the front seat beside Brett. She leaned through the crack in the seats and popped a knuckle into the top of Leonard's thigh.

"Damn, Hap, I was hoping she wasn't like you," he said, rubbing his leg.

"Me too," I said.

"What we could do," Leonard said, "is we could keep the money and shoot the guy in the head and give Farmer back his dog and no one would be the wiser."

"You talk some shit," Brett said, "but you wouldn't do anything like that."

"Maybe it's about time I did. I'm starting to look for retirement money."

"Retirement's a long ways off," Chance said.

"That's what Hap told me when I was thirty-five. Don't worry. We got plenty of time, he said. How'd that work out, Hap?"

"Not so well," I said.

WE GOT THERE three hours early. Come too close to time, the man making the drop might see us and figure we were planning on nailing him. We weren't planning that at all. We just had the microphones for insurance. Our plan was to make the drop and take Coco Butternut home to Farmer, who was waiting nervously. Then we would cash the check he gave us.

I parked a pickup I had borrowed inside the graveyard, as that would be how I was to haul the coffin away. Farmer said it was a full sized coffin and wouldn't fit in a trunk or backseat.

Leonard hid in the tree line beyond the graveyard, and lay flat. I insisted he not bring a gun. I was sick of them. Instead he brought a baseball bat. I brought a Yawara stick; a little stick nubbed on both ends, used by Jujitsu folks to strike and lock with. I was fair with it. Nobody was going to give me a job making an instruction video, but I could fuck you up with it, I needed to. I had it in my back pocket under my coat.

The days were mildly warm, but as winter moved in, some of the nights were a little brisk. I tugged my jacket tight and zipped it up. It was not only a chilly night, but a dark night, and maybe our kidnapper planned on that. I saw him or her coming in a large truck along the road toward the graveyard.

The truck wound down the road and the headlights flashed through the thin run of trees along the edge of the graveyard, and then the truck roared down the dirt drive that led into it, the tires large as those of a semi. If the driver was being sneaky about it, I couldn't tell it. I noticed the license plate had been removed from the front of the truck, and I guessed the back was the same. He'd probably slip them back on when he was out of our sight and continue on his merry way. The headlights were in my eyes, but there was enough residual light from them I could see the truck had been spotted with paint. Most likely a kind of paint you could hose off. It was too dark to know what color paint the spots were, and it didn't matter; it wouldn't be there long enough to make any difference should I want to identify it. The underneath paint was white, though, of that I was certain. Like me, the driver had showed up early, but me and my crew had shown up earlier.

I stood framed in the headlights for a moment and then the driver backed the truck and turned it into the graveyard and bounced across a couple of headstones, knocking them over, snapping them underneath the truck tires like peanut hulls. Rest in peace. The bed of the truck was covered with a camper, and it looked cheap, and my guess was that was more camouflage, and once the job was done, the driver would get rid of that too.

The driver's door opened and someone got out of the truck, and it was high enough from cab to dirt, they had to drop to the ground instead of step.

Then the driver came around in front of the truck with an odd waddle and stood there for a moment. I was certain it was a guy, and I could see he had a gun strapped in a holster on his hip. It was a big gun. He wore a black hood over his head. It had eye holes cut in it.

After a moment of staring at me, he opened the camper at the back with a tiny bit of a struggle, dropped down the tailgate and lifted the top of the gate, the part that had a little window in it.

He gestured for me to come to him. I left the satchel on the grave and went over. He took a small light out of his coat pocket and flashed it inside the truck. I could see a coffin in there. It was rusty looking and it was full size, far bigger than what you'd expect as the last resting spot for a weenie dog.

The man motioned for me to grab the handle of the coffin, and I did. I pulled, and when the end got close to the tailgate, he took the handle on that side. Lifted it out, and we set it on the ground.

He held out his hand, implying I should give him the money.

"I need to see what's in the coffin before I do," I said.

This was something I thought might get me shot for a moment. I wished now I had let Leonard bring a rifle, but then again, another reason I didn't want him to have one is he's not that good a shot. Not bad, but he might just as easily shoot me if things went asunder. Right then I thought we should have switched jobs. I can hit a dime on edge at considerable distance with nothing but a glint of moonlight shining on the dime. It's an inborn knack for someone who really didn't like guns at all.

We stood that way for what seemed long enough for the season to pass, and then he nodded his hooded head, and motioned for me to open the coffin. I could see where it had been pried open before, so all I had to do was lift the lid.

Inside there was a small cloth-wrapped thing that might have been the body of a real dog or a wooden cut out covered in cloth. The cloth had turned brown and was rotting in spots. There was a musty odor, but no real stink of death. The dog was long past that.

"I need to cut the cloth and see what's beneath it," I said.

A nod from the hooded man.

I took out my pocket knife and bent over and cut loose some of the cloth. The hooded man helped by shining the flashlight into the coffin. It looked like there were bits of dog under the cloth. Gray, loose skin, and in some places the withered muscles were visible. I decided it was a dog. Was it the right dog? I couldn't tell. I had done my part. I hadn't been hired as a forensic expert, which was a good thing.

As I backed off he put his hand on the lid to close the coffin. He had very small hands compared to the rest of him. He closed the lid, placed one hand on his gun grip, and the other he used to make a kind of gimme motion.

I walked back to the grave, picked up the satchel and brought it over. He placed it on the tailgate, opened it for a look, made a satisfied grunt, and closed the satchel and looked at me.

I hadn't moved.

He pushed the tailgate up and the upper portion down, walked swiftly to the driver's side carrying the satchel, pulled himself into the cab and closed the door.

I gave the truck a good onceover. Yep, spray paint spots, and I still figured it was water color. The truck rumbled and the lights came on, and then it moved away, swiftly, down the dirt and gravel graveyard drive on out to the asphalt road. There was a flash of tail lights through the trees, and that was it, he was gone.

LEONARD, BRETT AND Chase all had microphones, so they heard me, and in a moment Leonard came walking out of the woods swinging his ball bat slightly above the ground. I thought he looked disappointed. He hadn't had the opportunity to hit anyone.

A few moments later I saw headlights through the woods, and knew that was Brett and Chance coming around to meet us.

They stopped the Prius, got out and came over. Brett looked at the coffin.

"So that's all there was to it?"

"Yep," I said. "That was it."

"Silly fool paying for a dead dog, and we're talking one hundred thousand dollars, not a few hundred."

"I think it's sweet," Chance said. "It's not the dead dog, though I can understand that, it's about his mother."

"Yeah, Farmer and his dear old mother," Leonard said.

I went and pulled the pickup around, and me and Leonard loaded the coffin up, and we drove out of there with Brett and Chance following us.

AS WE RODE along in the pickup, I said, "I keep thinking who would know the dog was worth that much to him, and then, why all the mystery, why hire us to do it? He could have done what we did."

"Said he was scared," Leonard said. "So I got a feeling he might know who had the dog, and whoever it was wasn't in love with him. Knew he came to get it, they might take the money and shoot him in the head and that would be the end of it. But if one of us came, the kidnapper might not feel the need to kill anyone he didn't know. Just make the exchange and drive away."

"Could be," I said.

"What I'm getting is we're being made monkeys for something we don't understand, and I don't like that. This stinks more than a dead dog, brother."

"Dog didn't stink that much, actually."

"Well, it stinks to me. I don't believe that Farmer fucker at all."

"You are a skeptical man," I said.

"Find a place to pull over. I want to take a look at that dog myself."

"Already have. Musty. Loose fur. Mummified under the wrap."

"Pull over."

We were still out in the country, so I pulled over by the side of the road near a stand of trees next to a little, trickling creek.

We got out of the truck and the Prius pulled up behind us and killed the lights. Brett and Chance got out.

"Car trouble?" Brett said as she and Chance came over.

"No," I said. "Leonard wants to look himself. He thinks Farmer's story stinks."

"Really none of our business how true his story is," Brett said. "We've done what we were paid to do. I don't think swapping money for a dead dog is illegal."

"Unless you consider that whole extortion thing," I said.

"When you're right, you're right," Brett said.

Leonard had the tailgate on the pickup down and was tugging at the coffin, paying us no mind. I went over and took hold of the other handle and we set it down behind the pickup. Leonard opened it up. He had a flashlight in his pocket, and he was shining it around on the dog.

I said, "Okay. There is one odd thing. The dog is lying on a bottom that's higher than the real bottom. I didn't notice that before."

"I noticed it right off," Leonard said.

"I have your word for that," I said.

"Looks obvious to me," Chance said.

"Remember, I am your dad," I said.

"Yes, Daddy," Chance said.

By this time Leonard had lifted the dog out and placed it on the ground. There was a small hole in one corner of the false bottom and Leonard's finger fit in there. He lifted the false bottom out, and on the true bottom of the coffin lay a corpse.

I couldn't distinguish age, but enough of the flesh and features had survived that I could tell that it was most likely a woman, way the hips were set, way the wide edges of the bones cut through the rotting flesh.

Chase said, "Yuck."

"Damn," Brett said.

Leonard stepped back, pushed the fedora up on his head and looked at me. "What kind of dog is that, Hap?"

LEONARD AND I took the Prius. Brett and Chance took the pickup and drove the body to the police station. Me and Leonard went to Farmer's house. We might get our nuts in a vice over that with the police, even if the police chief was a good friend.

Farmer's home was inside a gate and there was a tall rock wall around it and great oak and hickory trees that might have been around when Davy Crockett died at the Alamo bordered on either side of a long, white, winding drive. We stopped at the gate and pushed the button on the device outside, but the buzzer we heard went unanswered.

I walked up to the gate and looked through. It was a big house at the end of that long, white drive. It loomed like a mountain and was as dark as a murderer's dreams.

"He was expecting us to deliver," I said. "So why doesn't he answer?"

"Might not like the answer to that question," Leonard said. "Grab a flashlight."

I went back to the car, got a flashlight out of the glove box and gloves for both of us. They don't call it a glove box for nothing.

Leonard walked along the fence until he found a thick vine that wound down off the wall. He took hold of it, and pulled himself up and got over the wall, nimble as a squirrel. I followed, doing the same, less nimbly.

We walked along the drive toward the house. A walk like that you damn near needed provisions. The shadows from the trees were as thick as chunks of chocolate cake. A chill wind was blowing hard, lifting dead leaves, tumbling them over us and across the drive in an explosion of crackles and pops. More leaves snapped underfoot like locust husks.

When we came close to the house we could still see no light, not even in the side rooms. There was a brace of dried winter trees and evergreen shrubbery all about. At the back of the house we found a door pried open, as if with a crowbar.

We pulled our burglar gloves on and nudged the door open further and slipped inside. It was a corridor, and we went down it into a room large enough to keep a pet pachyderm. I moved the flashlight around enough to see that the furnishings were expensive and the paintings on the wall seemed to be as well. The frames were all impressive. I got my frames at Walmart, so I might not be an expert.

I found a light switch and hit it and the lights came on. We wandered out of the main room and down another hallway and poked our heads in rooms along the way, switching lights on, but nothing jumped out at us. We turned lights off as we left the rooms. The hallway was very long and the walls on either side were covered in dog photos in nice frames; all weenie dogs. There were award ribbons too, lots of Best In Show stuff, and there was a large photo of Coco Butternut. I knew this due to my superior sleuthing skills and because underneath the photo which was encased in a gold frame was a metal plate that read: COCO BUTTERNUT, MY SWEETIE.

Last room on the left, Leonard turned on the light at the edge of the door and we went inside. More nice furniture, a fireplace you could have roasted a whole hog in. Farmer lay on the floor. He was not napping or watching a bug crawl across the ceiling, which was one of my pastimes. He lay on the floor next to the couch and there was blood all over his head and all over the floor and his head was a lot flatter than when we had last seen him. He hadn't just been smashed in the head, he had been worked over good. One of his arms was at an odd angle. His toupée lay in a puddle of blood, like a dead kitten.

"Now we call the cops," Leonard said.

We didn't need to, because no sooner had we walked back to the main room, than we saw flashing lights out the front window at the top of the drive. We stood where we were until someone got the gate open, and then three cop cars came rolling down the drive to park in front of the house.

I turned on a light that gave the front porch illumination, that porch being a giant concrete slab surrounded by shrubs, except at the steps which led down to a concrete walk. Leonard and I walked out there and stood with our hands loose in case the cops thought we were burglars or might be reaching for something.

Chief Marvin Hanson, our friend, got out of the head cop car and came over. "You guys," he said. "What assholes."

"What did we do?" Leonard said.

"Brett and Chance gave us the scoop, showed us the body, and we came here to talk to Farmer, and who do I find, but two salt and pepper assholes."

"That asshole stuff," Leonard said. "That hurts."

"You won't get to talk to Farmer," I said.

"He not home?"

"Oh, he's home, but someone in a very bad mood got here before we did and rearranged his head."

"Yeah," Leonard said, "he's all over the place in there."

"Shit," Marvin said.

SO MARVIN AND some of the cops, took a peek-a-boo while me and Leonard sat on the steps and shot the shit with one of the officers who had been assigned to make sure we didn't turn to smoke and disappear. The officer's last name was Carroll and last time we had spent any time with him was when Leonard was beating the hell out of a dog abuser and Carroll had been called to make sure Leonard didn't kill the guy. Leonard and Carroll got along well and they were laughing about this and that and pretty much cutting me out of the conversation, though I tried several ways by which I might enter into the discussion, only to find myself ignored or given short shrift.

I was still looking for my opening when Marvin came out on the porch and sent Carroll inside to do this or that. Marvin said, "Thing is, we get here and there's a dead body, and we got you guys, and this after making a trade at a cemetery for a dead woman in a coffin."

"We thought we were trading for a dead dog," I said.

"But you didn't call the cops when this blackmail was going on, now did you?"

"We did not," I said.

"Bad us," Leonard said. "You guys really would have cared about a guy trading money for a pooch corpse? That would have been like a priority?"

"Maybe not too much," Marvin said, and sat down on the steps by us. He shooed the other cops away.

"So how bad a trouble are we in?" I said.

"I don't think you did it," Marvin said, "if I take Brett and Chance at their word, and I do, but I'm not sure how a judge and a courtroom would take all this."

"He was our client," I said. "We came to find out why he had lied to us about getting a dog's body back, and there was a woman's with it. We wanted answers."

"You should have come to me," Marvin said. "I'm the law. We get paid to get answers."

"Okay. Here's a thought. Is there some kind of privilege for private investigators and their clients?" Leonard said.

"Only in the movies, boys. Only in the movies."

THEY TOOK US downtown but didn't throw us in a holding cell. We sat in Marvin's office with Brett and Chance. I had that feeling I had in grade school when the teacher made you write something or another on the blackboard multiple times.

"Here's what we're going to do," Marvin said. "I'm letting everyone go, and I'm saying you told Brett and Chance to tell me that you were going to Farmer's to do a welfare check, cause the guy in the cemetery looked dangerous, and you thought he might be a threat, and you thought you should get there and see he was okay. He wasn't."

"Could be the guy in the graveyard did it," I said. "We were farting around with loading up the body, stopping along the way to look in the coffin, and Leonard gave me bad directions, so it took us an extra ten minutes."

"I gave you bad directions?" Leonard said. "Bullshit, you can't follow a straight line if a string was tied to your dick and to where you wanted to go. Oh, sorry, Chance. No offense meant."

"None taken, but now I got that image in my head."

"Sorry again," Leonard said.

"He's not sophisticated like me," I said. "You'll have to forgive him."

Marvin said, "What I'm going to do is let you two go home, and then you're going to need to stay out of it. This could still come back to you, you know. No use adding fuel to the fire. Stay away from this."

We left out of there and drove our respective rides back to the office where Leonard put on a pot of coffee and got a bag of vanilla wafers out of the desk drawer.

As he did, he said, "These help me think."

"Sure they do," I said.

Brett and Chance drove up slightly after we arrived and came upstairs and into the office.

Brett said, "That was not too smart, boys."

"Yep," Leonard said. "Our usual."

"You know, guy in the cemetery would have to have been in a real rush to get there and do the job before you went over," Brett said. "I mean, he had to figure you might take the coffin right to him. He wouldn't know you were going to spend time looking inside or getting lost, so that would be some chance he was taking."

"Good point," I said.

"Means he probably had him a partner," Leonard said. "That means they get the money and while we're fucking around with Coco Butternuts and a corpse to be named later, he's got this other guy over there playing T-Ball with Farmer's head?"

"Butternut," I said.

"What," Leonard said.

"It's Butternut, not Butternuts."

"Whatever."

There were no more revelations in the offing that night, so we all went home. Later, upstairs Brett lay in my arms, her sweet breath close to my face, her hand on my naked thigh.

"You know that gets me excited?" I said.

"I'd be disappointed if it didn't," she said.

"That's why you let Buffy stay downstairs, huh?"

"She likes it downstairs now, since Chance is there. You know, we could do it if we did it quietly. I don't want Chance or Buffy to hear."

"Perhaps we could do it in slow motion," I said.

"I like slow motion," she said.

"Somewhere in the midst of it, though, we can move a little faster, if that's all right with you."

"Sure, but not too soon."

"Sounds like a plan," I said.

And it was.

I'D LIKE TO say with our great powers of deductive reasoning we figured out who did what and why by the next morning, but we didn't.

When I came downstairs Leonard had used his key to come in, and he was fixing breakfast and Chance was in her footy pajamas with dinosaurs on them, sitting at the table, sucking at a large cup of coffee. Buffy was sitting at Chance's elbow, waiting for her to drop something.

"I fed Buffy already," Leonard said.

"Thanks, bro."

"Leonard makes good coffee," Chance said.

"It's a Keurig," I said. "Anyone makes good coffee with that. You turn it on, the water heats, you stick a pod in and wait."

"Gave it my loving touch," Leonard said. "Waved my magic black hand over the pot. Gives it a kind of richness."

"I'm going to have to agree," Chance said.

Strands of her dark hair were loose from her hair tie and some of it clung to the side of her face. It made her look cute and young and made me feel even more fatherly, more protective. I had found out about her late in life, but I hoped I could be as good a father as I could from each day forth, but considering who I was and what I sometimes did, I had my doubts.

Leonard had gone all out with the cooking, scrambled eggs, bacon and cinnamon rolls. I ate a small amount of eggs and one piece of bacon and a cinnamon roll. As I got older weight and I fought it out on a daily basis. I won for awhile, and then it would come back and sneak up on me, climb into my belly and swell it. I worked out, but it didn't seem to matter, least not the way it used to. Fat was tenacious in middle age. I guess middle age is a silly term when you're fifty.

Brett came down in a bit. She was wearing sweat pants and a sweat shirt and her hair was tied back and her eyes were half closed. Time had stopped for her, and her aging was done in inches while mine was done in yards.

"I'll have a cinnamon roll and that's it," she said, and sat down.

I knew what that meant. I stood up from the table and got her a cinnamon roll and poured her a cup of coffee and sat it in front of her. When she had a couple sips of coffee, and had dunked her roll into the big cup, she said, "I think what we got to do is go to Farmer's business and see how things were there."

"He paid us to deliver money and pick up a coffin, and we did that," Leonard said. "Since he's dead, I don't see any more money forthcoming."

"That's never stopped us before," Brett said.

"You can't let it go either, can you?" I said.

"Nope," she said. "I don't like unsolved mysteries. I want to know who Jack the Ripper was and if Bigfoot lives in the woods. It's how I am."

"I'm curious," Chance said. "I know it's not my right to be curious about your work, but I am."

"Sure it is," Brett said, and reached out and patted Chance on the arm. "You're family, and we're a family business."

"I'm actually a reporter, and I need to go to work," she said. She stood up from the table and gave Brett a hug, went around and gave Leonard one, and then me. "I'm still curious though."

"We'll keep you in the loop," Brett said.

Chance went to get showered and dressed. When she left the room, Leonard said, "I think that DNA test was flawed, brother. She can't have come from you."

ME AND BRETT drove over to the mortuary and cemetery owned by Farmer. Leonard went to the cop shop to see if he could pry any new news out of his new friend Officer Carroll.

The cemetery and mortuary was off the main highway and down a dirt road. The road would be dusty in the summer, but for now, during the cool and dry times, it was solid and smooth. We wound our way between trees and pastures and came to the mortuary and cemetery. There was a section for humans, and one for animals. As we drove by, I glanced over the rock fence around the cemetery. Both sections appeared to be pretty full.

The metal bar gate was wide open, and we drove through it and stopped in the circular drive close to the curbing near the main building, which was a goodly size and at first glance looked nice, but at second looked worn around the edges; I knew how the building felt.

I had combed my hair and put on dark jeans and had tucked my shirt in and had on a nice jacket. Brett thought it might be the thing to do, going there. She thought they might see us as more professional. She had on a black business suit with a white shirt, and a business looking tie made of silk that she wore loose around the collar. The black boots she had on added to her height.

Inside it was a little too cool and it didn't look all that clean either. There was a lady behind a long desk. She was well dressed and a little plump, but it was a firm looking plump. Fact was, she looked healthy enough to turn over a truck and make it beg for gasoline.

We stood in front of the desk and she smiled at us. Brett said, "We were working for Mr. Farmer. Private investigators. We are doing some follow up, and would like to ask a few questions, if that's okay?"

The woman studied Brett, then she studied me, and then she leaned back in the desk chair and smiled a smaller smile than before.

"He didn't really operate this place, or had anything to do with it," she said. "He inherited money. Got a chunk of it every month and didn't so much as come in to see if the plumbing worked. It does, but not as well as it should."

"You sound a little unhappy with him," I said.

"I guess I shouldn't speak ill of the dead, but I couldn't speak about him at all until he was dead. Living, he had too much control here."

"Does that mean ownership has changed?" Brett asked. "I mean, the boss is dead so life goes on."

"Like I said, he was no boss. Just collected money. But he was the owner."

"Who owns it now?"

"I guess I do."

"Guess?" I said.

"The will is still being examined, but it looks that way. Jimmy quit having anything to do with this place five years ago, when his wife took off."

"Where did she go?"

"No one knows. She supposedly ran off with the dog mortician."

"How do you mortician a dog?" Brett asked.

"Not with mortician putty. We cremate them and we stuff them with chemicals after we pull out their insides, and sometimes we mummify them. That's extra. Got to be honest. The chemicals don't keep the fur from falling out, so some like the idea of mummification."

"Who in the world would be checking on a dog after it's in the ground?"

"It's the idea of it that the bereaved like. Frankly, it's nothing to me."

"You don't sound like a dog lover," I said.

"I'm not. But I can have them burned up or wrapped up for a nice fee."

"Question?" Brett said.

"Ask it," she said.

"First, to whom am I speaking?"

"Jackie Bridges," she said. "I guess I should throw in that I'm Jimmy's ex-wife."

"Ah, that's how you got in the will," I said.

"Nope. His mother did that. She never liked the second wife. I didn't either, but I wasn't married to her. I don't think Jimmy liked her too much. She looked good but wore badly."

"How's that?" I said.

"She was a bitch on wheels. Jimmy kept me on here after the divorce, and she didn't like it, but he wouldn't change it. Okay, not true. He couldn't change it. It was part of his mother's will that I could work here until I didn't want to or I died. The second wife was given a piece of it too, as his mother didn't want to alienate Jimmy. She loved him even if he didn't care that much for her."

"Why didn't he?" Brett asked.

"He wanted the entire thing to go to him. He went to a shrink of some kind and got told he had potty training issues, like not being able to shit right is going to cause you to make stupid choices. They got a lot of stuff for that problem in the drugstore. I don't think Jimmy minded me working here because that meant he didn't have to deal with someone new who didn't know the business, but the wife didn't work here, not a day, and still got a cut, and I won't lie to you, that chapped my ass. His mother, bless her soul, had it in her will that if she died I got half of the business and got to stay on. That was a big bite out of things for him. Meant his wife's share came out of his half, instead of what ought to be my half."

"So this places makes big money?" I asked.

"Nope. But she has a lot of other businesses and property rentals, so they make big money, and this is a nice foundation. Me and Jimmy and Betty Sue, that's the wife, all got a cut of that. Still do. This place does better than you think, but not as well as I would like. I haven't exactly been on the ball the last five years due to the fact Jimmy wouldn't allow me to make certain changes to upgrade. I had some power, like I said, but there were certain things I couldn't do without his permission, and he wasn't giving it. He didn't want anymore cuts to his money, and I couldn't convince him we could make more money by upgrading here and there. Way people are about their pets, hell, we could convince them to dress them in suits and sweaters that we provide. There's all manner of possibilities. One woman wanted us to have her dog put in capsules that she could take every morning until the dog was gone. Nice idea, but it's not sanitary and there are laws against it."

"One more question," Brett said. "Is it possible we could see where the body of Coco Butternut was buried?"

Jackie had a paper with all the graves listed on it, the names of the pets labeled. She gave it to me and I folded it up and put it in my shirt pocket.

"Just for the record, what's your view on cats?" I said.

"Don't like them either. Neither did Jimmy. His mother was the animal nut. I only like to eat them. Not cats and dogs, but animals like cows and such. Them I like with a side salad. Though, I don't know, you fix a dog or cat right, I might eat them too."

⟨~⟩c⟨~⟩

WE WENT OUT and around the side of the building, having been given permission to look about.

"She doesn't like cats and dogs," Brett said, "so she's on my shit list. But at least she's an asshole on top of it all."

"Her husband was probably a worse asshole," I said.

"Could be. But I don't like her."

"I think she was checking me out. You see the way she looked at me?"

"You have scrambled egg on your shirt."

"Oh. Right. I do."

Around back we looked out over the field of markers and stones.

"That's a lot of cats and dogs," I said.

Walking through the rows of animal graves we came to one that was nothing more than a hole and there was a large marker there made of granite. It read: COCO BUTTERNUT, CHAMPION AND FRIEND. There were no dates on it.

"Odd," Brett said. "Someone broke into the dog cemetery and dug up the coffin and carried it out and no one noticed."

"It is off the main road," I said.

Brett nodded. "Yep, but it would have taken awhile."

"Looking at the grave, I think they used a backhoe."

"So he drove up on a backhoe?"

"Seems unlikely, but not impossible."

Brett nodded again. I could see she was working some ideas around in her head.

A young man walked up. I hadn't even noticed him. "Can I help you?" he asked.

He was tall and thin as a shovel handle and had a wad of blond hair on his head that looked to have been styled into a bird's nest, something for a condor to sleep in. I had never seen hair bunched up like that and so blonde it was nearly white. He had a nice face though. At first he looked young, in his thirties, but the more I looked at him the older he looked. Forty or so, I reckoned.

We explained what we were about, and when we finished he nodded.

"Of course. Look about all you want."

"So, obviously," I said, "you work here."

"I'm Jackie's son."

"So you're Jimmy's son too, I take it," Brett said.

"I'm Scanner. Mom named me after part of a science fiction book title. She was married before Farmer, but her husband, my father, James Sundrey, died when I was about ten."

"Sorry," I said.

"No sweat. He was a son-of-a-bitch too, just like Farmer. Can't say I miss him. He was about as fatherly as an earthworm."

"I take it earthworms are poor parents," I said.

"That's my take," he said.

"So what's your job here?" Brett asked.

"Whatever is needed. I have my own business. I make prosthetics and sell them."

"Your own company?" I asked.

"Online, but I make good stuff. Have some patents. I'm catching on. I'm anxious to get out of the pet smoking and wrapping business.

"There's another branch to the cemetery, though," I said. "People."

Scanner pointed. "It's over there, but I don't care that much for smoking or burying people either. What I want to do is end up going to Hollywood, make special effects for movies. I can really do some cool things with prosthetics, you know foam, make-up."

"Good luck with that," I said.

"Thanks," he said. "I guess I'll go now. I have to attend to a few things. Hey, you got something on your shirt there."

"Scrambled eggs," I said.

"Ah."

"Question," Brett asked. "When you do deep burials, and it looks like Coco here got a nice one, how do you dig the holes?"

"Backhoe," Scanner said. "We keep it in the shed."

And he pointed to the back of the cemetery where there was a long, high-roofed building made of aluminum.

A LOT OF things were clicking as we drove away, and we discussed them.

"Okay," Brett said. "The ex-wife didn't like him, and her son didn't like him, and there's a backhoe in the shed, and yet, it doesn't quite come together."

"If she knew there was a body under Coco Butternut, she didn't mention it."

"Because she knows she's not supposed to know. She's in on it, I bet you an enchilada dinner on it."

"What kind of enchiladas?"

"Focus, Hap."

"You brought up enchiladas."

"I also brought up I think she's involved in all this."

"Guy that drove that truck was a big dude, not a woman and not as skinny as Scanner."

"Still think she's involved. Maybe we should come back tonight and look in the shed?"

"So they have a backhoe?" I said. "Scanner said as much, and a business like this would have one."

"Yes, but maybe they have a big truck as well, like the one that brought the coffin. As for the big guy, maybe they got a third partner. It could easily be that way."

"If they're the ones did this," I said.

"I don't have the proof yet," Brett said, "but I think we can bumble along until we do based on that assumption."

"I'm a good bumbler."

"You and Leonard both," she said. "It makes me proud."

ME AND LEONARD made an appointment with
Marvin while Brett went to the office to hold down a
chair in case a new client came in, one that wasn't dead
and was paying. What we were doing was now gratis,
but damn if we wanted some skunk to use us as a way
to get money and kill Farmer.

Day before Leonard had visited with Officer Carroll
and asked him a few questions, things that could help us
nail the murderer. I called Marvin and let him know we
hadn't been good, and that we were snooping, just what
he'd asked us not to do. But when I told him what Brett
and I had learned at the mortuary, about the financial
arrangements and the will, it stirred his interest.

"I kind of hate you guys," he said. "You never do
what I ask."

"We're like teenagers," I said.

"Assholes," he said.

Marvin was seated with his feet on his desk and
there was a steaming cup of coffee on the desk as well.
He had a file in his hand.

"Officer Carroll seems to be talking out of school,"
Marvin said.

"He might have been led to think I had your permission," Leonard said.

"He might have been led that way, might he?"

"Yep," Leonard said.

"Alright, to hell with it. Maybe you boys are actually onto something."

We seated ourselves in chairs in front of the desk and Leonard perched his fedora on his knee.

"Can we have some coffee?" I said.

"Go to the break room and get it," Marvin said.

"Don't you have minions?" I asked.

"For police work."

"Get mine too," Leonard said. "And if they have any cookies, vanilla in particular, bring some of those."

"We don't have any cookies," Marvin said.

"If I ran this place vanilla wafers would be a constant."

"If you ran this place there'd be a lot of fat cops," Marvin said.

"I'm not fat," Leonard said.

"You're a freak of nature," Marvin said.

"Actually," I said, "he's showing his age some. He recently had to drop ten pounds."

"So did Hap, and he could drop ten more."

Marvin eyed me. "I was thinking twenty."

"You're probably right," Leonard said. "He doesn't work out as much as he should."

"I have other things to do," I said.

"He's lazy," Leonard said.

"Well," I said. "That too."

"Okay," Leonard said. "About that coffee, Hap. Stir my sugar in good. You know how to fix it."

"Fuck you," I said, and got up to get the coffee.

When I came back, Marvin had pulled his feet off the desk and tucked them underneath it. He had the file open in front of him.

"I'm assuming that file has to do with the death of Jackie Farmer's first husband," I said.

Marvin smiled. "You arrived at the same place I did. Here she is with two husbands, and they are both dead and with their deaths money is to be made. The first there was a fat insurance policy, and with Farmer she made money as a business partner as well as a wife, and when they split, she made money just as a business partner. But Farmer's mother liked Jackie, and it seems that gave Jackie a home court advantage. Then Farmer got a new wife and that led to new complications, until the new wife disappeared. Way I think Jackie had it figured was she was in a good position to get it all, due to Farmer's mother making her a big dog at the mortuary. With Farmer and his new wife gone, she would own the mortuary, the cemetery, the whole business. And there's the insurance on Farmer too. The mother put in her will should Farmer die, a sizable amount of the insurance money she had on him would go to Jackie. That's a really large incentive for murder, you ask me."

"What Jackie told us," I said. "She didn't try and hide it. Though she left out that whole advantage for her due to murder."

"I had to look around for a file on her first husband's death, and that took some work, and it's interesting in what's not in it," Marvin said.

"Like the dog that didn't bark in the nighttime," I said.

"Like that," he said. "The first husband started feeling bad and ended up in the hospital, and the doctors couldn't figure the problem. I think if we dig him up we'll find out what the problem was. I'm guessing poison. I think this Jackie is an operator. She didn't kill Farmer while the money was easy, even after the divorce, but at some point my guess is she thought it was a good idea."

"And Farmer's wife?"

"That might be a bit more complex. Farmer didn't like her much, and there had actually been three or four calls to the police by the missing wife, saying he was abusing her. And there was the whole business about her fucking around with someone, and then suddenly she's gone and so is the guy. Old Police Chief thought it was kind of suspicious, but he couldn't prove anything and Farmer just went on being Farmer."

"And Jackie went on being Jackie," I said.

"Right," Marvin said. "My guess is she somehow knew what Farmer did, kept it in her back pocket. Why not? She wanted to be rid of the wife too, and then one day she gets the bright idea she can get some money for the body, and then get rid of Farmer too. The time was right with the mother dead and her knowing where the body was and the will lined up to make her golden. She could sit around with her feet up and a fan blowing up her dress for the next ten years and not have to hit a lick at a snake."

"What about her son?" Leonard said.

"Checked on him," Marvin said. "Has a jacket. Had a few little notes added to it on a regular basis." Marvin shifted to pick up another folder, opened it. "All of it petty stuff. Peeping Tom, stealing women's clothes at the laundry mat. Stuff like that. He got caught on that one and they found selfies of him wearing stolen panties on his head. His history of panty hats was right there. He's one of those dreamers thinks he's going to be something he's too lazy to be, a special effects artist or some such."

"He told me and Brett just that thing," I said. "But wearing panties on your head is a long way from murder."

"Course," Leonard said, "we don't know the dead woman in Coca-cola Butterasses coffin is Farmer's wife."

"We should know that in a few hours," Marvin said. "I got some guys in Tyler owe me a favor, so they're making DNA tests. Can do that stuff quick these days, they take a mind to, and there aren't a bunch of cases lined up in front of it. That's where the favor comes in. But I think we know who it is."

"And probably there's a dead boyfriend somewhere too," Leonard said. "You know, the wife is underneath Coconut Butterballs, then there's a good chance that boyfriend of hers is lying under another dog out there. Farmer killed them, the ex-wife threatened to expose the murdered wife, got some money in the deal, then got Farmer whacked. It's a tight idea, you think about it."

"I know I like it," Marvin said, "but thing is, even with one body on hand from the graveyard, we got to have a bit more reason to dig the other body up."

"Why would they care if you dug it up?" I said. "They got what they wanted, the money and Farmer dead. Farmer most likely put him there, so why would they bother not letting you check the graves out? It just puts more guilt on him, I'd think."

"Well, something is bothering them," Marvin said. "We asked and they said we would need a warrant."

"That paints things a different color," Leonard said. "Ah, I got it. The other body, maybe Jackie helped dispose of it. Maybe she helped in the murder of the wife too."

"Yeah, but still all things point to Farmer, not her," I said.

"Jackie may have played her hand too far, blackmailing him and killing him on the same night," Marvin said. "But what I'm thinking is she's thinking there's something in that other coffin that points back to her. My guess it might even be something she can explain away, but if she can get rid of the body, dig it up, cremate it and put the boyfriend's ashes in the flower bed, she's laid out smooth as silk. I think Farmer had a good idea who stole the body. He may not have known she knew he did what he did, but at that point, someone blackmailing him with his wife's corpse, he had to have an idea."

"Why he sent us," I said. "Had it figured right. They wanted to kill him. He thought he'd be all right if he stayed home, that paying her off would save his neck, but it didn't."

"Which brings me to a thought. You see, as Police Chief I have certain restrictions. You know, my hands are tied on some things. But I'm thinking if someone who didn't have those restrictions was able to find some evidence, maybe not too illegally, but you know, real soon, and it was something a Chief of Police could use, and those people, two guys say, were to present it to me in a fashion where I could find out about it in a good way, and I could use it in court, wouldn't that be nice?"

"So, you're talking about us?" Leonard said.

"Maybe," Marvin said. "You know, there might be something at her house, inside, or somewhere. Something like a big, white truck, which would be a nice place to start, though not quite good enough to finish, but what if they had four hundred thousand dollars under the bed in Farmer's satchel."

"That might be hoping too much to find," Leonard said. "Even for those two guys you're talking about."

"I think Jackie is too smart to just poke that satchel under the bed," I said.

"True," Marvin said, "but you never know, and you know what, they might have hidden it at the mortuary, but you see, I got this warrant I got to get, and the best I can do is get it tomorrow, and I'm not entirely sure the judge is going to give it to me, not in time, anyway. He's kind of stickler. But I'm thinking I get enough to pull them in, and get that Scanner fellow in interrogation, I can dangle a fine set of panties in front of him and he'll spill the beans."

"You'd dangle panties in front of him?" Leonard said.

"No," Marvin said, "I think he's the weak link in all this and he'll spill with little more than a cup of coffee and me giving him a stern look, but I thought that part about the panties sounded good, so I said it."

CHANCE, BEING PART-TIME at the newspaper, had a day off from work, so we gave her the job of going out to the cemetery road and parking close to where it emptied into a highway. There was a parking lot there that went with a grocery store of some size. She could sit there in her car and see the road clearly.

There was a back way out of the cemetery, but it was a long way, and it stood to reason they would use the shorter route. If they did, if Scanner or Jackie left the place, went home, went anywhere, we would know because Chance would use her cell to let us know. She had on a baseball cap and a loose shirt and shorts and sandals and had her lunch with her in Brett's STAR WARS lunch box. I think Chance liked playing detective. The idea of it anyway, but after lunch, if she was still sitting there and waiting without news, she might be less interested.

It didn't take much research to figure out where Jackie and Scanner lived. Scanner still lived with his mom, which was no surprise, and he had a place in the backyard. We knew that because we drove over there in Leonard's pickup and walked along the walk and went straight up on the porch. We had on khaki clothes and caps that could have fit any city worker doing any kind of city job, jobs that might require someone to go from house to house, or do work inside, say on a gas line or a phone line or electrical problems, plumbing perhaps. We could make a lie go in any direction we needed to.

At the front door Leonard took out the lock picking kit and messed around for awhile, and when he clicked the lock, he discovered there was a dead bolt as well and a chain. He locked the door back with his tools.

If they had the front door locked like that, it meant they locked it up inside and went out another way. We strolled casually around the side of the house, next to some ill-kept shrubs, and finally we were at a chain link fence with a gate in it. The backyard was high in weeds, but there was a walk along the side of the house and it came to where we stood at the gate. The gate had a padlock on it.

There was an old travel trailer in the yard with grass grown up around it. Behind that was a large shed and the pines in the yard on either side of it had dropped rust-colored needles on the roof making a thick carpet. We could see a padlock on the shed door from where we stood. The sunlight dappled through the pine limbs and leaves and gave the place a camou-flage look.

"Like their privacy," Leonard said.

"Lot of people do," I said.

Leonard worked the padlock easy with his tools, and we went inside the yard, closing the gate behind us.

"Bet you the kid lives in that travel trailer, and that's his workshop out back for the things he sells online," Leonard said. "Also betcha he doesn't sell much online. I think that's just his story so he doesn't seem like the loser he really is. Grown man living with his mother like that, they always got excuses, usually about how they're taking care of Mom, but it always seems to be the other way around."

"You used to live with us," I said.

"You shut up."

We pulled on gloves and started at the back door of the house. Leonard cracked the lock quickly, and went inside. It was marginally neat, about the way mine and Brett's place looks before we clean up for company. The air had a cinnamon smell. There wasn't much of any great interest, some photos on the wall of her and Scanner. One of them he had a mask of some sort pushed back off his face and it nestled on top of his head. I couldn't make out what it was supposed to be, but my guess was he had made out of foam or plastic. His face beneath the pushed back mask was young and happy. My heart hurt for him. Once he thought he'd have more to life than a trailer in the backyard, maybe have a Hollywood career making masks and such for horror movies.

In that same photo Jackie had her arm around him and was smiling. She looked pretty good. Thinner then, healthier, less angry. Maybe she had just poisoned her first husband and was happy about it. Around her neck was a necklace with a dangling pendant. It was fairly large and silver with a green stone in the center.

We made our way through all the rooms. Leonard stopped to use the bathroom, and then we slipped out back and locked the door again. We went out to the travel trailer. It had a padlock on the door. Leonard used the lock pick and in a moment he clicked it open.

"I'm getting good at this," he said.

Inside, the place looked to be more a nest than a home. Clothes were strewn about and the sink was full of dirty dishes and the place smelled like old food and mildewed clothes and too much jacking off.

"Yeah, Scanner lives here," I said.

"Guys like Scanner always got a story about how they're going to become something or another, but they aren't going to get there, and they know it," Leonard said, flashing the light around.

"What about us?" I said. "We aren't exactly living high on the hog."

"It's a higher hog than we used to live on, rose field work and such."

"Yep. We're growing up."

We went through the travel trailer which took us about two minutes. We searched for another ten or so, found some nudie magazines under Scanner's mattress.

"I wouldn't touch those too much," Leonard said.

I put them back under the mattress. There was a little TV mounted at the foot of Scanner's bed and a stack of DVDs, all popular movies with lots of explosions and car chases.

We gave the place a bit more of a look, but all we found were some shit-stained underwear on the floor and a drawer full of clean women's panties.

"Scanner's head gear," Leonard said.

We went out and snapped the padlock into place.

"Nothing exciting here."

Out back we got in the shed easy. That lock might as well have been a piece of thread tied across the door.

There was dust in the place and it was moving about in the flashlight beam. There were tables with oddities on them, pieces of this and that. There were superhero masks and chunks of foam, artificial limbs.

"Okay, he really does make prosthetic limbs and such," I said. "And they look like they're pretty good quality."

"I know you, Hap Collins. You're thinking if he'd just had the right encouragement he might not have become a sad asshole who lives with his mother."

"Well…"

"Let me tell you something, he decided on his own to be a sad asshole who lives with his mother. Sometimes there are just assholes, Hap."

I shrugged. "Maybe."

There was a window at the back of the shed and it looked out on a little road that ran up to a fence that bordered the back yard. There was a truck camper on the ground out there. I recognized it. It was the one that had been on the back of the spotted-up truck that night.

I heard a sound at the back of the shed, but when I changed my place and looked where I thought it had come from, I saw nothing. Cat probably. I was getting jumpy.

"Look here," I said.

Leonard looked out the window at the camper.

"That's the same camper cover that was on the truck that night," I said.

"Lot of those out there," Leonard said. "And they all look alike."

"That's it," I said.

We looked around and found more of the same, and then in a closet we found a set of legs and arms and a torso. Not real ones, but prosthetic ones. There was a foam head with eye holes and a black hood was pulled over it.

"No wonder our man at the graveyard walked funny," I said.

"Scanner was wearing this shit." Leonard said.

"Why he looked big and his hands looked small. He had this on to disguise himself, made him look more formidable. With the hood on, gloves and clothes, it being night, I couldn't tell. I just thought he walked a little funny."

Leonard pulled one of the legs out and used his hands to bend it at the knee. It bent easy.

"Feel it," he said.

I took it. It was light as a feather. If Scanner had the whole thing on it would have been a little cumbersome, but I could tell it was easy enough to move around in it if you practiced.

"Okay," I said, "how do we get it so Marvin can come in here and check things out?"

"I was thinking we set the travel trailer on fire and call Marvin and the fire department."

"So they put it out?" I said. "Stuff we need is in the shed."

"Leave it to me."

Leonard took out a burner cell. We got so we carried one each on us or in our car or pickup.

A moment later the call was made.

"Hey, Marvin. This is Leonard… Of course that Leonard. Listen, there may be a trailer on fire out back of a house on Prichard Lane, 303, and it might need to be put out, but you know, the shed behind it, you might come with the fire department, just in case you might need to snap the lock and look inside to see if anyone's in there. Fire might spread."

Leonard listened, then closed the phone.

"Okay. He's coming in twenty, so let's find a way to set a fire in the trailer."

Outside of the shed Leonard put the padlock back in place, and then he picked the lock on the trailer again. Inside, Leonard pulled the curtains over close to the electric cook stove and placed the end of one of them over one of the burners. He filled a frying pan with cooking oil and put it on top of another burner and heated up the grease. I understood then. I got some frozen French fries out of a bag in the refrigerator and poured them in the grease, and we let that heat until the potatoes were popping, then Leonard placed the hot pan on the curtain over the other burner and turned that burner on. In a moment the curtain caught and the flames ran up the curtain and along the wall. I poured the oil and potatoes from the frying pan onto the stove and the hot burners caught the grease and then the top of the stove was on fire. We went out of there and locked the door. It wasn't that we thought Scanner would think he forgot and left potatoes on the stove, but it would sure look that way to the fire department at first glance.

"What if it doesn't catch good?" I said.

"Say some driver drove by, saw smoke and called it in but didn't want to leave their name. That driver wouldn't know how bad the fire was, only that smoke was seen. Hell, it might be out by the time the fire department gets here, but they got to go on and take a look, don't they?"

"They do, indeed."

Away from the house we walked along the street and glanced back. No smoke was drifting from the backyard. The fire might be out, but it was the excuse Marvin needed. He'd have the fire department break in there and then he'd say he thought he smelled smoke coming from the shed to, and they'd break in there too, or that's how I figured he'd do it.

In the pickup I took off the work cap and Leonard did too, slipping his fedora in place. I called Marvin on my burner.

When he answered he said he was already in route. I said, "I was you, I'd look close in the shed out back. Fact is, I'd look in a closet there where you'll find the disguise of the guy that brought us the dog and we gave the money. There might be a camper shell out back like the one the blackmailer was using."

I explained a little more to him, and then I picked up my personal cell and called Chance.

"They still there?" I asked.

"They didn't come out this end."

"You can go home now."

"Good," she said. "I'm out of coffee."

WE THOUGHT IF Marvin found the prosthetics and I said that Scanner was wearing that rig when we gave him Farmer's money, it would be good enough and over with.

But it wasn't like that, and of course, thinking back on it, there was no reason it should be.

Marvin came over late afternoon, and sat at the table finishing off coffee with me and Leonard, Chase and Brett.

"We can't go to the DA with what we got. We know the little bastard was in on it, probably his mother too, but we can't prove it. The rig he had, all you can say is you think he was wearing it. You didn't think that until you saw it in the storage building, and I can't say you were there, as they would get your asses in trouble for breaking and entering, and I kind of encouraged that. I mean the fire is suspicious as it is, but it did get us in the shed and we did find the prosthetics, so it's something. But, not enough. We didn't even take the stuff or them into custody. We got a free look, and that helped, but that's the end to it. Have to give me more, if you're up for it, and frankly I don't know what more is, but if you say I asked you for more, I'll deny it."

"Like the way you didn't ask us in the first place," Leonard said.

"Just like that," Marvin said. "Here's the thing, this isn't really your problem, and you could let it go. It's really my job to figure this out."

"Don't have sympathy for Farmer," Leonard said, "but I don't like us being saps in all this."

"I don't like we were handing Scanner money and in the meantime, Farmer was getting his brains knocked out, and right now, I'm figuring Jackie did that herself," Brett said. "If it was Scanner at the graveyard, then Jackie was most likely the muscle. She looked stout enough to swing a tire iron or a bat and make it count."

"You got a bother about it all, then you got to come up with more proof," Marvin said. "And let me tell you, that setting fire to Scanner's trailer was an iffy idea. That could have gone way wrong."

"But it didn't," Leonard said.

"Still, try and play it a little safer, okay? We had Jackie and Scanner come in and fill out some papers, you know, and the general consensus was that juveniles broke into the trailer and set the fire."

"That isn't far off," Brett said.

"Ha, ha," I said.

"Wow," Chance said. "Meeting people in a graveyard to swap money for a corpse. Murder. Arson. Bad language from my father and uncle, a stakeout. I certainly have been living a sheltered life. I like this one better."

AFTER MARVIN LEFT we mumbled about this and that for a bit, but didn't come up with anything constructive, but after we poured ourselves more coffee, Chance said, "I got an idea. It might not be a good one, but do you want to hear it?"

"Right now even a bad idea might sound good," Leonard said.

"In our case, they usually do," I said.

Leonard said, "Wait a sec," got up and pulled out the stash of vanilla cookies we keep for him in the cabinet and put them on the table. He opened the bag and stacked a half-dozen cookies in front of him and started dipping one in his coffee. "All right, I'm ready," he said.

"Okay," Chance said. "From what's been said, it appears Jackie is worried about someone digging up that other body in the graveyard. She told the law they had to get a warrant. Right so far?"

We agreed she was.

"She may not be hiding anything. That might just be good business, trying to keep the graves intact. She wouldn't want her customers to think that whoever, animal or human buried there, will be excavated at the drop of a hat, so she makes a stand. But if she doesn't want them digging graves up for another reason, could that reason be she knows there's something in the other grave, the one with the boyfriend in it, that might somehow tie her to the murders?"

"Like what?" I asked.

"That's where my plan falters a bit," Chance said. "I don't know. But that could be it, couldn't it? And if we got to the grave before she did, that would be good, because if there's something there, she'll try and get to it before a court order goes through. She might fight it off a few days with a good lawyer, but she's got to know in the long run the law is going to win out on this one. Those graves are going to be investigated. She may have dug up the one she needs to check already, but you know what I'm thinking is she'll wait until late tonight so as not to be so conspicuous. She's stirred up by today's events, and by the law's request to dig up some graves, so she knows that fire wasn't merely an accident. She's bound to suspect the law did it so they could snoop. She knows they want in that graveyard bad, and she's got to figure that court order is coming soon, so that means she's got to get to it and hide whatever evidence she believes might be in the coffin. She would most likely want to go there late at night to make her move, dig the grave up when fewer people might notice. What we need to do is beat her at her own game."

"Well," Brett said, "it's some kind of plan."

WE DIDN'T GO there when it was fresh dark, but we tried not to wait too long. When the sun was solid set and the stars were high and bright, we drove out there.

Brett was the only one of us that could drive a backhoe, as she had worked for the street department when she was young for a summer, and claimed she could make that machine purr, shit, and call other machines bad names. I was her partner in the venture.

Leonard and Chance went in Leonard's truck, parked at the same place where Chance had waited to keep a look out before. Since the lot was empty, they parked close to the building there to look as if the truck might belong to the owner.

They had a good view of the turn off to the cemetery as long as Jackie or Scanner came from that direction. It seemed the most logical path for them to take. It was the most direct route.

Driving past the cemetery, me and Brett scoped it out. There were lights in the front building and behind that was the dog graveyard, and beyond that was a long building where the backhoe should be and there was a tall booger light on a pole.

We parked down a ways and walked back. I had a crowbar in my hand and a flashlight in my coat pocket. Brett had a flashlight in her hand, one of those big heavy cop things, but had yet to turn it on. We could see clearly enough. It was a bright starry night and the moon was near full. The air was cool and crisp as a starched collar and the air smelled like pines and it tingled in the nose and throat. As always, doing something like this, I was nervous and excited at the same time. In the sky bats were flying, chasing insects. You could see the bats well enough, and if you looked hard you could see the insects flying in the celestial light with the bats swooping down on them.

When we got to the cemetery the gate was locked. It was one of those tall, iron bar things with the bars pointed at the top, and there was a big lock where the gates closed and hasped together. I got out my lock picking kit and couldn't do shit with it. Brett took the kit and went to work. It took awhile, but she got it. We swung the gate open slightly with a haunted house creak and slipped inside and pulled it closed with the same creaking sound. It locked when it snapped together.

The wall around the cemetery was made of worn stone and mortar. It wasn't real high, but it was damn sure solid. It had most likely been built by the WPA during the Great Depression. Where we were had certainly contained something other than a cemetery back then. I think I had heard somewhere about there had once been a school in this location, but it was torn down in the sixties and eventually the acreage became the cemetery.

We eased along the drive, past the front building and the outside light that was on a large telephone pole, and then we started across the graveyard toward the long, high, storage building.

It wasn't that long a trek, but out there in the bright celestial light it seemed a long ways. I felt as if I were on a hike to Antarctica. You could see us easy from the road, and in fact maybe from the moon.

"If the keys aren't with the backhoe," Brett said, "we get a shovel and I can watch you dig."

"Hoping for keys," I said.

The shed had a padlock on the great doors that were chained together. Brett made quick work of it with the lock picking kit, and then I pushed the doors open and we went inside. Brett took her light out of her pocket where she had tucked it, and turned it on, flashed it around the shed. It was really more a warehouse than a shed. The roof was tall and the room was wide. On the walls we could see all manner of gardening tools hanging, but the thing that interested us was what was in the center of the building, resting on a concrete floor like a dinosaur. A yellow backhoe, and an orange bulldozer, both of good size. They had cabins surrounded by glass. I guess if you're going to scrape ground and dig holes, you needed the right equipment. More interesting was a big white truck, and even without its spots, I felt certain that was the truck I had pulled the coffin out of. I went over and looked at it and was even more convinced.

"You know we are breaking so many laws right now," I said.

"Yep," Brett said. "I have become as gangster as you."

We looked around a bit and I took some photos on my phone. They might not be legal photos in a court of law, but they would certainly show Marvin that mother or son owned a big white truck and the camper in their backyard would conveniently snap together over it.

Brett climbed up on the backhoe, slid back the glass door and looked inside.

She called down to me. "Key's here."

"And you're sure you can drive it?"

"I said I could." She was already settling herself onto the seat.

"I know, but that's been a long time ago."

"It's like giving a blow job, you just don't forget something like that."

"Ouch," I said.

"By the time you and I got together I had perfected the art."

"Ouch again."

"It's not like I was doing it for pay."

"Ouch even again."

"I'm not making this any better am I?"

"Not much."

Brett turned the key and the backhoe growled to life.

"Climb on up," she said.

THE BACKHOE HAD a lot of controls. Brett buckled her seat belt. That made me nervous. I didn't have a seatbelt. Why did a backhoe have a seatbelt?

Brett released the parking brake and shifted the transmission into forward. The bucket was already up. She drove us through the open doors and the backhoe rumbled us out into the cemetery.

It seemed obvious to us that if there was another body out there under a dog, it would most likely be next to the grave of Coco Butternut. If Farmer had to get rid of the boyfriend too, it seemed natural and simple that he would do them side by side and be done with it.

Brett stopped the backhoe, said, "Which grave are we digging up, one on the right or left of Coco Butternut?"

"It's a crap shoot," I said. "Go for either."

Brett chose the one on the left and started working the scoop. She had a delicate touch. I knew that already, but it was interesting to see it applied to a backhoe. She dug down a few scoops, and we were already there. I could see a coffin.

I climbed down with my crowbar and jumped into the grave and stuck the bar under the coffin lid and pried. It came open easy. There was a dry, musty smell. I could see right away that the dog inside was resting on the bottom of the coffin. I climbed out of the hole and stood there, shaking my head at Brett.

She went back to work. Two scoops and she scraped the top of the coffin in the other grave. I got down in that grave and did what I had done before. The dog lay high in the coffin and I used the tip of the crowbar to move the false bottom back. There was a human corpse underneath.

I looked up at Brett and nodded.

No sooner had I done that than I heard a roaring and looked toward the sound and saw the bulldozer come out of the warehouse at the end of the cemetery.

"Shit," I said.

Brett leaned out the side of the open backhoe, said, "You better come up."

I clamored back inside the backhoe.

"Looks like our watchdogs failed," Brett said.

"Whoever it is, they came in another way," I said. "Leonard and Chase wouldn't have missed them."

"I don't intend to fight a bulldozer," Brett said.

I figured the bulldozer driver had come in to do what we thought they might. Dig up the grave, but we had beat them to it, and then they had fooled us by coming earlier than we expected. That's how it goes. You can't assume shit.

Brett whipped the backhoe around and we started heading for the closed and locked gate. Bulldozers run faster than I thought they might, and it was closing on us. As we came closer to the gate, Brett said, "Hitch up your nuts. We're going through."

"The gate? Really?"

"Easier than the wall."

She gave the backhoe all the juice she could, and away we went. She used the bucket like a knight's lance. It hit the gate and there was a noise like someone skinning a cat, and then the gate buckled a little, but held. We were pushing so hard at it the tires began to smoke. I looked back.

The bulldozer was coming fast, whirling onto the drive, and inside its glass cabin I could see Jackie. She had a look on her face that I can only describe as goddamn unpleasant.

The back of the backhoe lifted up and the front tires smoked like a bonfire. Brett changed gears, and the rear end settled. She went at it again. The gate groaned like someone who had just had their knee capped, and then it snapped open. Brett gunned it through, but the bulldozer was as tight on our ass as a hemorrhoid. It hit our rear end and pushed us through and off the drive and onto a patch of grass beside the main road.

Brett turned the backhoe deftly. We bumbled across the patch of grass and then we were shooting onto the road, the dozer banging against the back of the backhoe as we did.

Another move by Brett, and we swung wide and to the right. The dozer was surprisingly dexterous in its moves, but not as swift as the backhoe, and with that maneuver we got away from the dozer, at least by a few paces.

We raced away, but the dozer was back on track and coming fast. There was a crack in our windshield where it had hit the gate and cold wind came through the crack to add to our misery. I looked back.

Behind us, the dozer dropped its blade so that it skimmed over the road. I knew what that meant. Jackie was going to try and scoop us from the bottom and flip us. Seemed like a good plan that I didn't want any part of. I felt a turd loosen inside of me and thought it might be surfacing soon.

Down the road toward us came a pickup. It was Leonard and Chase. I didn't know why they were coming, but they were. Leonard's truck was bent up in front and I could see there was a third person in the cab with them.

Chance was driving the pickup. Leonard was sitting on the passenger side, and then they were so close I could see who was in the middle. Scanner. It wasn't so much that I could make out his features in detail, but I could see him well enough to know it was him. They were heading right for us at what one could politely call an accelerated rate of speed, and we were on their side of the road. So, there we were, the backhoe flying along as fast as it could go, the bulldozer right on top of us, and Leonard's pickup heading straight for us. It was like me and Brett were about to be made into a sandwich between them, and then—

I HURT A little.

I could smell gasoline.

I woke up in a dry ditch and I could see the stars through the boughs of a pine that draped over me. I couldn't remember how I got there or why I was there, and I don't know if I even knew who I was for a moment without checking my driver's license. That's when I realized I was lying in a ditch. I didn't normally lie in a ditch. Why was I in a ditch?

And then I thought about Brett, and that got me moving, slowly, and then I thought about Chance and Leonard, Jackie and that goddamn bulldozer, and by then I had rolled over and was pushing up with my hands and climbing up out of that ditch. It wasn't a deep ditch, but I felt so damn weak it might as well have been me scaling Mt. Everest.

Chase was driving right at us, and then she veered, and when she did, Brett tried to take the backhoe to the right, but the bulldozer climbed up our butt, and the backhoe did a crazy slide and there was the sound of metal against metal and the sound of our machine blowing a tire; it was like some kind of weird music for the damned, and away the backhoe went, spinning.

When it came to a stop, the dozer hit the machine in the rear, crunching it a little, since it was pushed up against that brick wall that ran for a long ways at the edge of the cemetery. We really hadn't gotten that far.

I remembered the dozer blade being lifted and being smashed down on the back of the backhoe like a giant fist, and then I remember the glass cab shattering and me flying. My moment as Superman, but the landing was my moment as a mortal. Next thing I knew was I was waking up in that ditch. As I climbed out and stood on the road, I moved my parts to make sure they were all there, and they seemed to be. Nothing fell off. I could feel blood seeping at the knees of my pants and my hands were scraped and so was my face.

The dozer had the backhoe pushed across the road and up against the long stone fence, and it was pushing it and crushing it, and I could see Brett still in it, slumped over in the shattered cab.

I tried to dart toward the dozer, found I wasn't darting too well. In fact I was limping like I had one foot in a bucket of solidified concrete. I saw the crowbar I had been holding lying in the road and picked it up.

I glanced right and saw Leonard's pickup was turned over in the same ditch I had been lying in, only a little farther up the road. Gasoline was leaking out of the busted gas tank, and my heart sank. Then I saw Chance slip out of an open window, and behind her came Leonard. They were staggering about like drunks, but they were all right. That's all I needed to know. I didn't give a flying damn about Scanner. I came up the back of the dozer and scrambled up it as it eased back for another run at the backhoe. My pain seemed to go away. I was on top of the dozer and I could see Jackie. She had her back to me and she was shifting gears and the dozer was lurching forward.

I swung the crowbar, hit the back glass and the crowbar bounced back and nearly came out of my hands. I swung it again, and saw Jackie turning her face toward me. A warrior's face. She gunned the dozer backwards and I nearly lost my footing, but I bent low and held on. The dozer's movement paused, I came up and swung the bar again. The glass fell like chunks of shiny ice. I went through the hole to get at Jackie, ripping my shirt and cutting my arms a little on the broken glass. Jackie was up and out of her seat now, and she was like a wildcat. She grabbed me by the throat and rammed me backwards.

We went through the gap in the glass and I felt my arm being ripped by the glass, and then we were tumbling over the back of the dozer and falling to the street.

Jackie jumped astride me and started swing her fists, knocking my head from side to side like a piñata. I had lost the crowbar during all that, but Jackie found it. She stopped hitting me long enough to reach over and grab it and then she lifted it above her head with both hands and was going to drive the sharp end into me. I drew both legs back quickly and put my heels inside her thighs, close to her waist, and kicked with all my might. She went back and the crowbar came down and hit me without design. It hurt, but not as bad as it would have. I grabbed the bar, and then me and her were on our feet. She was a strong woman and I was an injured weak man. We both had hold of the bar now, and I was trying to wrest it from her, or at least keep her from whacking me with it, when a fist flashed out and hit Jackie in the side of the head, hurtling her head over heels without the crowbar. I was left holding it.

Brett was there. Her face was scratched and she was bleeding from the mouth and nose.

"Fuck with my man, and you'll have the undertaker wiping your ass," she said, and kind of collapsed against me. I held her. She was breathing heavily, but she seemed all right.

"It's okay," I said.

"Of course it is," Brett said.

I looked at Jackie. She was out cold.

Leonard limped over with Chance.

"That was some punch," Chance said. She was all out of breath and hopped up on adrenaline. She was vibrating.

"I brought that with me from hell," Brett said, righting herself.

"Scanner?" I said.

"Good thing they own a cemetery," Leonard said. "It's going to make his burial cheaper."

"How did you know we needed you?" Brett said.

"Didn't," Leonard said. "We saw Scanner drive by and we started following him and he made us and started driving fast, and we thought, well, shit, he knows we're here, so Chance drove faster. Scanner lost control of his car and put it between two trees. I don't know how he did it, but he spun out and flew off the edge of the bar ditch and landed ass backwards in it, his car about three feet off the ground. It was like a goddamn circus trick."

"It was kind of funny," Chance said. "Well, I hate he got killed later, I think. But it was kind of funny right then, that car in a tree."

"You been hanging around Leonard too long," I said.

"I pulled him out of the car and asked him a few questions that he didn't want to answer," Leonard said, "then I interrogated him with my knuckles and he started to talk. His mother had come the back way, she always went that way, he said. A road we didn't even know about. Jackie was going to do what we thought, brother. Dig up the body. She thought she lost a necklace in the coffin. Hadn't thought about it in years, just knew it came up missing, and then when Marvin wanted to dig up the coffin, she got to thinking she had been wearing it the night she saw Farmer bury the coffins. She went out there and dug them up to see what was in them, saw the bodies, realized it was good for her, them being dead, and later she had Farmer's crime in her back pocket. And then she thought maybe that's where her necklace had gone. Had come off in one of the coffins when she was prying the lids open to look inside. Thought it had come loose of her neck and fell in one of them. It didn't turn up in the wife's coffin, so she figured it had to be the boyfriend's."

"It's like I thought," Chance said. "Well, mostly."

"Yep," I said. "Thing is, I looked in that coffin pretty good. I didn't see a necklace."

"It's probably under a couch somewhere," Brett said, "and she should not have bothered. She was golden and didn't know it."

I looked at Jackie sprawled on the road like a collapsed puppet. She hadn't so much as twitched a muscle.

"That was one hard lick," I said.

"She wakes up, I'll give her a fresh one," Brett said.

MARVIN CAME OVER later that night after we had all been arrested, and then released, except for Jackie. I don't know there was enough evidence to nail her even then, but with the death of Scanner—he ended up with Leonard's truck radio pushed into his chest when the truck flipped—Jackie had had enough. She wanted to come clean. She told Marvin everything, filled in the gaps. Marvin told us we were going to have to pay a fine for digging up the cemetery, commandeering a backhoe that didn't belong to us, and breaking into a closed cemetery, but considering Jackie's confession, he figured we'd come out all right. We might have to pick up trash along the highway for a few days in orange jumpsuits and pay a fine, but that was the worst of it.

"I'd get to wear a jumpsuit?" Chance said.

"Darling," Brett said. "Don't be too proud."

Here's some of the stuff Marvin told us. It isn't all that new, some was obvious, some we guessed, but he had the facts from Jackie now.

Farmer buried his wife and her lover after killing them. Jackie was working late one night at the mortuary, looked outside and saw Farmer using the backhoe, digging up graves. She started to go out and ask him what was up, but hesitated. She watched from behind a shrub on the back walkway out of the mortuary, and watched him dig the holes, climb off the backhoe and pull the coffins out of the holes. They were cheap coffins, too big for dogs, really, but they were bought in mass and were cheap. They were light metal. She watched Farmer pry them open, take out the mummified dogs.

She watched him pull some bags out of the back of the truck, let them smack on the ground. He pushed them into the coffins and fitted in the false bottoms he had prepared, put the dogs on top of those, closed the lids, and pushed the coffins back in the holes, covered them up with the backhoe. Tomorrow he could claim he was doing a bit of cleaning work around the graves, and that's why they looked freshly dug.

A few days later when Jackie knew Farmer was out of town, one night actually, she dug up the graves and found what was in them. She covered them back up. It was to her advantage to have the wife dead, and now she had a secret that Farmer was unaware of. She literally knew where the bodies were buried, and as we also suspected, she waited until the time was ripe to play that card.

It hadn't quite worked out the way she thought.

Jackie also admitted she killed Farmer. Still had a key to the house from when they were married. He never changed the locks. She waited on him in a closet with a baseball bat, and surprised him. It took her one lick to knock him down, and then she finished him with more than was necessary. There was a lot of rage in that lady.

Scanner had been in on it, of course, but Jackie claimed he didn't know she was going to whack Farmer, only knew about the money part of it.

It didn't really matter. Scanner, innocent of murder or not, was as dead as those who were under those dogs.

SOME TIME HAS passed. The cemetery is closed down now. No new customers will grace its grounds, human or otherwise. I drove by there the other day for no reason at all other than I wanted to.

I parked at the front of the cemetery and walked through the gate, which was still open and wrecked from us ramming through it. I walked over to Coco Butternut's grave. The dog had been reburied there by the county. Farmer's wife and the wife's boyfriend had been hauled away by relatives who finally knew where their kin ended up.

I looked down at Coco Butternut's grave. Thanks to that mutt we had caught a killer.

"Good dog," I said and went back to the car and drove away.